Bill Callahan

LETTERS TO EMMA BOWLCUT

DRAG CITY | CHICAGO

Drag City Web Address: www.dragcity.com

Printed in the United States of America
Library of Congress Control Number: 2010930681
ISBN: 978-0-9820480-2-3
Cover design: Jaime Zuverza

Third Edition

*This book thanks
Connie Lovatt
for giving it life.*

*And Damian Rogers
for giving it shoes
and a little hat.*

In the pursuit of further knowledge Joe was subsequently struck by Philadelphia Jack O'Brien, who had been hit by Bob Fitzsimmons, who had been hit by Jim Corbett, Corbett by John L. Sullivan, he by Paddy Ryan, Ryan by Joe Goss, and Goss by Jem Mace.

THE BOOK OF BOXING
W. C. Heinz and Nathan Ward, editors

PART ONE

The world had gone quiet around me. The deafness fell like a heavy snow. Slow and steady. Since then I have been waiting for the crunch of footsteps to join me. Using my senses in that conscious way. And I always hold a silver micrometer (rhymes with thermometer). If I've had enough to drink, it gets dropped in a pocket. Then a little more to drink and out it comes again.

I heard those footsteps. I turned my head and you were there. At that party. I was the one whose date was a micrometer.

I went under the air of being dragged out. In truth I had probably put as much thought into the party as the people who threw it.

I could talk about your hair or my studies. They are intricately connected. And that is what struck me about you. I am dominated by my work. When I saw it growing out of your head, I had to write you.

I couldn't talk to you but I had to write you.

Your reply arrived like a cockle dropped by a hungry gull. Do they even make cockles anymore. I put the letter on my kitchen table then ran a bath. As in the olden days, cleanliness hasn't been presenting itself as an option. I bathe to stall for time.

I sat down clean at the table. My neighbor leaned out his window, sniffed and called across, *Are you baking a chocolate cake.*

Your letter twisted its hair. The first you have ever written me.

I called back, *No.*

We'd never met and he was there staring at me and flexing his nostrils. I couldn't believe how close he was. I said, *I made some toast awhile ago*, because he wouldn't move away from the window.

There were cake pans on his counter and a bag of flour. I think he was the one making a chocolate cake. He stood up straight and wiped his hands slowly on his apron all the while watching me. He looked like he was about to cry. It was his Cake Day and I had no wish to dampen it.

There were chips of what looked like ceiling deep within your envelope. Mine disappeared last winter. Turned wet and silver then bronze and fell in soft, gloppy chunks. And I still haven't done anything about it.

I heard the drip starting at 4:00 A.M. from my bed. I had been living under seventeen inches of snow, melting for who knows how long.

One of my goals is to not ask questions as that implies that this has all happened before and I am merely asking you to tell me how things went. Which isn't to say I don't believe in destiny.

You have every right to ask me what I do, but I don't think there's a name for it. I study the Vortex. I use micrometers mostly. Such work has already divorced me from so much and yet I undergo it all with the exact opposite in mind.

I am hoping you are the missing think thing. Your letter filled the hole in my day like a key.

Turn it.

Munching around, champing at the bit. I was chomping at the bit until I found out it was champing. Getting out of the house to stop the film loop in me. The picture is tangled and the sound is strangled. That there is nothing in this for you is something that occurs to me now and then. I can forget anything.

But something commands me. Is it you from another mouth. One I am not yet sure you hear. Come closer in that deafening snow. There is hot desert rock beneath.

I walked around the block as if to walk around a blockade and then sat in my car reading the paper. I'm charged up. Energy. Neighbors are bugging me. Irritable. Right forearm tingling. My micrometer hand flutters like a shutter in an empty camera.

I spent last night sifting through a ten-round snoozer. The one feller whose forte was fighting on the outside, the other whose forte was on the inside. Neither of them throwing anything. Even the tolerant ref wanted it to end. You can't always fight the fight you want to fight. But god I wanted the uppercuts to connect.

At the heel end of day, I need my glass of wine. Christmas lights for the brain. In lulls we assess the gulls. I don't want to destroy anything. But I want to know what I can destroy. I am possessed by the conviction that I need you like blood needs a vein to get from one place to another.

I think sealing wax is what you mean. I don't think there is such a thing as ceiling wax.

I remember everything from the party. You seemed driven. You kissed all of your friends hello and goodbye even though you only stayed fifteen minutes. I noticed your hair didn't shine but absorbed light like the Vortex. Then you opened your mouth and I wanted to kiss your teeth. Or eat one or two like mints.

I could tell you were wearing the outfit that was your uniform. Mansome shoes with no socks. I later saw the same shoes on a flock of nuns. You didn't need me at all. Your eyes were the room. Your lower body was Mystery River. And your voice was several voices.

I wanted to hold you until I heard one voice. I stood without intention of moving and realized we see every punch coming in a boxing movie but in real life we miss a lot of them.

I was on a brisk walk for bourbon thinking about what you wrote. The city was a greenhouse. The past bloomed like a grotesque orchid. I was walking through my life of twelve years ago. I saw a dead ringer for my best friend of that time.

Where is he now. Our friendship went into the cool woods.

I've searched for him. I hired people. One person. An alcoholic.

My head snowed with dog-eared memories as I walked cradling the bourbon baby in my arms. The Chinese restaurant's neon sign read *Arroz Fritos Chinos*. A window display featured a clear glass toilet bowl. I saw myself in it. I hoped these weren't the events I would remember twelve years from now.

A boy ran past me with no pants on. His mother chased him carrying what he'd shed. Maybe the boy was my old friend and the mother was me.

About our visit—I'm not mild-mannered but you may want to bring a book.

I talked to my grandmother on the phone. She is getting up there. I'm not sure if she heard a word I said. She has moved into a nursing home. Because of the lapses.

It crossed my mind that my letters are all about me and not you.

I would hope that you pay me the same respect.

One of my favorite things of all time is when an animal keeps company with a different species. It's often a duck. Maybe you should get a duck for that library you work in. No one would complain. Ducks belong in libraries.

I had my teeth cleaned by a squat, youthful 50-year-old with hair so orange it was blue. Her hands were the smallest I'd seen on an adult. It was as if she were bred for the profession, the way she perched on the chair with her watch in my mouth. My choppers are a mess and everyone is angry about it. The receptionists even accept my money angrily.

Being in those dentist chairs gives one time to think about one's feet. I have a theory that feet should not be different temperatures, that it causes upset and even illness. In the winter, if I can only find one sock, I wear none.

You getting a coat "cut down to size" has put many images in my head. All of them probably inaccurate. Like you fell asleep as an adult and woke up as a child and dragged all your oversized clothes to the tailor.

Work is something I must ease back into. I can't really explain what I do. If you watched me it would look like almost nothing. I've been told I look like I'm petting butterflies in the air.

It's good you wrote about lack of sex. That's what's really troubling me. That film loop I mentioned a couple weeks back isn't blank, it's wall-to-wall copulating. I push my way through the entwined bodies as I walk.

It could just be a yeast infection. You should get it checked out. Don't make your old man make love to a doughnut. That is, if you two are still going at it. It's been hard for me to tell.

I've got a head full of air, too. Unfocussable. I can not unblur my eyes enough to read a micrometer. A drink centers me but I usually make myself wait until at least 9:00 P.M. for that. Or 8:00 P.M. Whichever comes first.

Then spiders tussle on the page with my hand as referee.

I looked at a book I have with the solar system on the cover. It was on the floor and I opened it with my bare foot. I looked at the earth nestled there among so many unfamiliar objects—a duck among the cows—and decided it was a blessing to keep trying.

I think I'm getting better at loving people, but I have no idea where that thought came from. I'm getting better at loving your boyfriend. Whether or not that's what he is.

There's a street fair being set up right in front of my house. Rides, cotton candy, Kill The Clown, the whole bit. It's like there's a constant reverie going on outside my house. A gaudy flashing dream that only stops when I go to sleep. I pull out of my parking space straight into a traffic jam. Inch along, look around. I had no idea where I lived.

This city is a mess. City, teeth.

You leave and return so easily. I admire the cadence of it. I want to go out more but a nation's army needs me to wash 50,000 blood-splattered uniforms first. In the river, on a rock.

The Vortex mocks.

I'm bored alone and bored with my social options. Sometimes the weekend comes too soon. You don't get a chance to miss your friends.

I moved my bed into the bedroom. It seems healthier to be ready to accept visitors even if none are scheduled. Having the bed in the center of the living room was like sleeping on a moored skiff.

I get more accomplished with this new way of sleeping.

There is probably little to nothing in your library about my profession. Yet it is an old discipline. Invisible, omnipresent. Not so much a secret as too delicate to withstand common scrutiny.

The other night I had to endure Mina Bunn. She kept telling me what I need. She teased me about the Vortex life. She's so self-centered, her criticisms of other people are only criticisms of herself. If she goes out and doesn't see you, she thinks you must not be going out. Still we let her come around, and I've been trying to figure out why. She's pretty. That's part of it. And she always has something to say.

Always.

But enough about me. What about you. You've been iceberg-tipping-it lately. I need to know more about this man of yours. Baron Von Pirate Pants.

And I hope each morning you wake like a bird in a nest and fly without a thought.

It may have read that way, but I wasn't scoffing at anything. I am possibly lonely. I was trained to turn loneliness into laziness. The problem being I am not working hard enough to relax with a pure heart afterwards. I test and re-test the things I already know. That said, I'm definitely going to get drunk with someone soon. Who the lucky duck will be I don't know. And I will lay off the cracks about your man. I think we could still visit each other as friends though. If you wore that yellow jacket and black tights and yellow shoes you would probably sting someone before the night was through.

A wasp landed on my arm some time back and dug in. I looked at my arm, watching the whole thing from Position No. 3, the position for watching television. I hollered louder than I knew. A mixture of pain, surprise and indignation. But then I thought I saw the Core and got real quiet. It occurred to me to provoke the wasps for further insight, to let the venom be my instinct. I went out into a field, rolled my sleeves up and waved my arms but no wasps in sight.

Funny you should write to ask if I was thinking of boxing. When I sat down to open your letter I thought, I haven't thought about boxing for a while. I've felt too busy to go to a match. It was possible, it just didn't seem right.

We are always making choices and then we go to sleep. At separate times.

Work progresses. The work is all around us. All I need to do is turn my head and I am, in effect, working. But if I don't turn my head....

Your encouraging letter never arrived.

Robin was the name of my last live-in girlfriend. Robin Bangs. I was some sort of refuge to her. It was a decent house atmosphere. She used to put a doily on top of the fire logs. And we didn't even have a fireplace.

I didn't want to admit I was aware of what she was doing. Which is alright. But you shouldn't let someone seek refuge in you. With is alright.

Understand that this is just talk, as I know you will. And it is unformulated and I might take it all back in a minute if I talk long enough. Which I'm not going to do.

She hated my work. Furied by it. Would flail into the room stabbing at ghosts and lashing at nimbus fingers that floated and pointed ways, decimating them into a faint haze. She's also real nice. I connected with her quick. Still, a baby that wants to be babied. I'm not into that, unless the girl is sick or has had a particularly bad day. I don't feel I can trust her. So I have to put her in a place where it's not necessary to do so.

Why am I talking about this so much. Because you asked I guess.

Got to go finish dropping rags into a sack.

I learned that you can get bruises without external contact. Struck by something trying to get out from within. Please use a pre-existing orifice. You did tell me about that wide bruise. I remember thinking it must've looked like the ocean from an airplane. And I spent some time writing you up a mock prescription form for gin and tonics, but I threw it away.

I got blitzed last night and wept like I was being whipped. Robin asked me to never call her again. The ceiling and floor are so thin I was half hoping that one of the annoying women from above or below would hear me and come up or down from their beds into mine. They never came, but I could hear one of them creaking the bedsprings with her lifted neck and I took it as an act of commiseration.

I'm empty from bawling. Feel like I need to take a wife. And my hands smell like gunpowder. Happy birthday, by the way.

Work teeters. I keep the instruments in good order through disuse. Silver discs in boxes with mother-of-pearl inlay and velvet lining.

I think it's a good idea not to give a fuck. I find myself suddenly not giving one. And I'm well aware that you can reshelve the books in flawless alphabetical order while still not giving a fuck. My good gracious lady, my light behind the rabbit's ears, I fall at your feet and kiss your mansome shoe. Please ignore the flask exposed in the process.

I had been sleeping well in night's abandoned factory. But last night I turned and turned. I've condensed the act. I spin around three times in the air and land. I got out of bed and made my way to the kitchen in the dark and shoved two spoonfuls of peanut butter into my mouth. I once saw a man on late-night television say this helps you sleep. That was twenty years ago and I think of it every damn time I see a jar of the stuff.

I understand about your man/non-man. I picture a shadow receding to reveal more darkness.

As I remember it, Robin asked if she could kiss me and I said no. She begged off later saying she just wanted to kiss me the way one kisses a big dog. I didn't believe it until recently.

I spent the last two evenings with the same bunch of jokers joking. Movies and restaurants and being entertaining. It was fun but now it's done. Robin is still in mind but if she doesn't want to be, then she shouldn't be.

I hope you are finding time to write me. Take off your mitts and write me. Or does the sight of your demitted mitt negate the mitt mittiness of mitt all.

I talked to my grandmother. Her forgetfulness is spreading. She said my favorite game when I was a kid was to turn my old crib upside down and pretend I was in jail. She said I would sit in there all day pretending to play a harmonica and if someone walked by I would yell, *I'm ready to see the judge!* And, *Don't make me go into that dark shack alone!*

Why don't you come here. I wish I had a nicer place to offer you, but why don't you come here. I will be moving soon anyway. Before those winds come that cover all in dirt.

Sorry to hear you're in a tornado. Just because someone has a need for monogamy doesn't mean they necessarily practice it. There is honesty in laying with whores. I've never had a professional massage. I think I owe myself a couple thousand.

I've heard numerous times that your favorite horror journalist is a regular at cathouses. I get so dry when I'm working. Like a desert that needs an encompassing rain. Not a good analogy, but I guess I'm saying I can see it somehow. From the branch of a petrified tree.

But is that it for you and the Baron. It's hard to tell. You always talk like it's over but when I suggest such a thing you're quick to correct me.

My television died. The picture squinched to a blurry cube and then it was gone. I almost got up and went straight to the TV store, like putting out your last cigarette while heading for a fresh pack. Found out I was bottle- not breast-fed. Was chic at the time. Me and sister Fig got the bottle while oldest brother Thomas got the breast. Now he has a wife and three trefuckingmendous kids. Fig is more swooping. And well, you've seen the way I treat people.

You resolved that fast. Not sure if that's a good sign or a bad one.

This day seemed like it could have gone either way. The sky half blue, half gray. When I looked again the gray had lost to blue (a Civil War sky), and then it rained a cloudless rain.

The place next door is vacant. Did I tell you. Cry-baby baker is gone. Now it's just painters hanging out the window with the occasional cig. I wonder who's going to move in next and if they're going to leave their curtains open as much as Chef Sensitive. If they are considerate of my feelings, they will. That is the problem with the world today. No one thinks of his or her neighbor.

Nice story about the grouch behind the counter. I was thinking, as I read it, how insurmountable some people are. But then you proved me wrong, you got him to smile. I am so often wrong but find it more rewarding than being right. I had bad experiences with clowns as a kid, too. These ones had guns. What makes certain alcoholics become clowns.

I once spent five days on my knees scrubbing the black fat between the tiles in my cabin at HQ. Ponderous labor was what I was after. One of the docs came in to yell at me. I regretted the hug I had given him on arrival and slept with a hat on for six nights.

You ought to write me about what you're going to write me about and some other stuff, too.

You are the reason I get out of bed. To tell you that I have gotten out of bed. Yours are the only questions I want to answer. I live to pocket all the question marks, as many as I can, in your life. To discard them discretely when you're not looking.

I get called in to HQ a few times per year and sometimes go on my own accord when I want to be in like-minded company. If they call me, I have to go. I'm expecting to go soon and am looking forward to it. They examine me and my data. It usually lasts three or four days.

I shaved off my beard and a lot of my hair. I'm facey now. I look like Eleanor Roosevelt. In her prime, at least.

I crave some stimulation but not in the form of a sloppy-chewing dinner guest. I need to hear and respond to questions of varying complexity. I need that placidity of the give and take.

It's hot there, isn't it. I hope you're either keeping yourself pale or tanning until completely dark.

Don't tell me you're the kind of person who always thinks they lost a twenty-dollar bill. There is a certain type of person who always thinks they lost a twenty-dollar bill. Fig. You see the twenty at the restaurant. The way it's crumpled it looks like it won't be around long. The way she fishes it out of her purse and sets it to the side while looking for something else. You can already hear the words. You leave the restaurant. She is searching through her bag...*I think I lost twenty dollars.*

I'm moving soon. I'll send you my new address when I have one. It won't be far.

It was good to get something from you longer than a few lines. So you're alone now. I'm sorry. I didn't think I would be, but I am. I could open the floodgates and write for pages but that's not the right thing to do.

There's darkness in neglected work. I don't tell people about it as it's tiresome to have a friend playing this card too often.

But there's an upside, Upside. I found a place. When I talked to the landlord on the phone, there were birds chirping in the background. I think it'll be a good place. Say, maybe now would be a good time for you to visit.

The first few hours of the day here lately are just trash. Bundling up the alpha waves with a message for the gamma.

I read about the importance of fresh foods and then went out and bought a lot of canned, dried, boxed stuff. But I read a diatribe against honey and threw out the jar I found in my cupboard, which I had bought on a special trip to buy healthy honey. Apparently it's Satan's blood. It's only a hair better than sugar. And it's a pre-digested food, like milk, which is bad.

I've been jumpy lately. People and shadows make me jump. Is that a nutritional deficiency.

Robin used to hate to see me eat. I chewed too long for her taste. One day I figured it out. She had put two and two together. All that chewing! It was the food that was keeping me alive!

I've been doing some sketches when I go to boxing matches. I make them for you. Only now they could be too personal.

Maybe I misread the milk and honey thing. I thought milk was pre-digested because it was made from something that passed through nine stomachs. But I guess the stomach leads to the udder as much as a stomach leads to breasts. Funny you should start off your letter correcting me. Lucky for us both it picked up after that.

I'm sorry to read about your skin disease. Does it hurt to smile. Read on.

It's true. There were a few other bits I could have sent you. I was holding back. And now I'm blanking. I haven't been drinking. Sober evenings of reading. The nights are so long and quiet without drink. I can read 400 to 500 pages. I'm reading a book where everyone calls each other fat. It somehow seems like the ultimate existence, what we should all be striving for.

I was in a sour mood for eighteen hours but then it lifted. I'm not sure what is underneath, Tubby. I am taking care of everything. Had a biopsy on a mole. It was fine. Going to have it sewn back on, Pudgeball.

It has been warm here lately, one good thing. And the warmth is tangible, has a shape — a long tapering tail I follow into the cool night.

When I moved, I unearthed the diaries I kept for ten years. I sat and went through them and they were a worthless burden to own. People will say it's tragic I threw them out, but I know it isn't. I don't feel I have a true perspective on anything. So I can't cast light on your hallway of shot bulbs.

I didn't ever decide if Robin would be a good wife. There are many unanswered questions about her. She didn't make to answer them, which both pleased and troubled me. They say marriages work better if you don't know the person too well. Maybe we should stop writing each other posthaste.

I know I haven't mentioned work much lately. If I have a hammer in my hand, I'm a handyman. I broke up my old kitchen table and neatly inserted it in the trashcan. It was a ten-dollar lopsided table I had been carting around for six years as if it were a family heirloom. It was never any good. It's funny how things can become their opposite.

I bought a big bag of potatoes and it's growing eyes like crazy. Other foods rot. Potatoes want to see. Huck Finn's funeral.

As I unpack my stuff I find lots of things I'd like to send you as gifts. Just about everything I own. I turn the TV on but stare out the window at the sky and tree turning yellow-gray. I fear there is no work for me here but I speak too soon.

I look forward to sleeping each night. The air is cool and it often starts to rain around 2:00 A.M., breaking the heat and singing me to sleep. And I drink my tequila as if I'd be letting you down if I didn't. I hope you're enjoying your mugs of rainwater as much as ever. And that the pain isn't too much to bear.

I feel good. Appreciative of my days and the air I breathe. I found a place here with fights. Went last night and the remarkable moments were few. But I didn't mind as the boxers didn't mind. We were all just there for it, which was fine. The highlight was one feller going down for the second time, squarely beat—the ref holding him down with a loving hand on his chest. The fighter saying, *I'm clear, I'm clear.* The ref shook his head. The downed man said, *Let me up, I'm embarrassed.* And that bald admission cut through everything. I could barely hold my head up after that for fear of making eye contact with him. I must be the only son of a bitch in the crowd with tears welled up at just about every fight I see. A boxing match is like a wedding. Oh, it's so beautiful.

Just before starting this letter I read for twenty minutes in the park. But I felt vulnerable. Little nut things fell into the grass behind me and squirrels were rustling, folding down the blades. I kept thinking someone's coming to hit me in the back of the head.

I like your theory that the sounds that surround us sculpt the shape of our head. So I will sit in each empty room now feeling my head shift like a sand dune in a steady breeze.

Seagulls give a hopeful air to any place. Make you feel like you can't be too far from land. Do churches still ring bells. I can hear a train far away late at night. A religion, also. Mostly I hear the German Shepherd feller next door, whimpering in the morning mist. And there is a raven that caws. They can be friendly. I read a book. They like to collect things for no known reason. And roll in the snow past the point of cleanliness.

The clouds here are specific. White outlined with lavender. Headed east. Accept them with my compliments. I saw an eagle flying so so high in the sky. Sometimes I wish we were an eagle.

I joined a boxing gym, paid for a month and only went once. I'm afraid I'm not going back. I got paired up with a 17-year-old kid who looked 14 and was trying to get in shape for boot camp. There was a murderous lawyer wailing on the heavy bag. I saw the Vortex black between his shoulder blades. Blackness breathing out of him. His face was an afterthought, a smudge, barely defined. The pro fighters went about their business like birds who knew where the best food was.

Isn't there something hateful about going out on dates. The last date I went on, the girl (a ballerina!) picked me up in a huge truck with wheels that set it four feet off the ground. She wouldn't stop saying how sorry she was that she insisted on picking me up, but she couldn't trust anyone's driving, afraid of having her legs crushed. I told her I didn't mind, but she kept talking about it.

So I remain the feller in the restaurant who reads waitress name tags as if they were actress credits in a movie.

People come around ringing the bell here a lot. Like Old America. Offering some service or other. Or possibly casing the jernt. All things spawn from an even place and reside in equal measure. To deny an emotion weakens the opposite emotion. I went to the fights. I was a pill. I went with a friend. First time not alone. Not sure if I like it. I prefer to concentrate. And we had to sit far away as he made us late and we missed the first few rounds of the initial fight.

See, I was a pill. Still a pill.

I usually have two or three deeply moving moments there. Not this time. Was it the quality of the boxing or the fact I wasn't alone or that I was farther back. The waitresses were showing a lot of cleavage and I tried to ignore it to the detriment of my match-watching skills. When one is denied, its opposite is weakened. Or was my love for the game weakened by denying the displeasure caused by my tagalong.

I have a black and angry-looking growth. Went to go get it cut out today. I was nervous. Taxicabs are lawless places so I swigged freely from a water bottle filled with vodka on the way over. I was happier because of it and would have been happier yet if I'd had more. Fuck every living thing. Don't tell nobody.

HQ is on a peak pocked by a single crater—the mouth of the Vortex.

I'm not allowed to bring a companion. But I can invite guests to the conventions. Maybe I could take you to the next one. I always assume people know this stuff already since I'm constantly immersed in it. I forget that it is not what most people spend their time thinking about.

I appreciate your image of me as a man who keeps in shape despite habits. But the desire to exercise only comes to me in times of extreme adversity—the biting cold or the bludgeoning hot. The street dogs were steaming so I got my jump rope and went down the backstairs into the alley that leads to the church parking lot. I started asking myself questions, as all the big ones come when I'm about to get my heart up. I'm tired of the theme where the man just keeps rolling on. Jumping rope is an offering. I mean, my body is an offering when both feet are off the ground.

It was late, and there was a milky light in one of the church windows. There were two cars in the lot and I wondered what a couple does when alone in a church so late at night. I wondered if my jumping rope meant anything to anyone but me. I could have married Robin easy.

I thought of the gods and bricks that built this church. The spire had a little ball on the end like a trailer hitch. I looked over at my apartment and saw it was made of the same brick. Maybe it was made with the leftover bricks from the church. Or vice versa. I thought about spitting. I was sweating. There was no reason to spit. I spat. I pictured my heart jumping from the roof of my apartment to the roof of the church and then slowly sliding down the tiles, trying to hold on. Then reaching the edge and dropping to the ground at my feet.

I'm not really interested in religion or history or science or mathematics or psychology or politics or geography. I feel I am above them all, except geography. Geography is above me for now.

Robin was a strong swimmer in the strong water. Much stronger than me. And she constantly wanted to race. I hated to lose in my soul. I would always try to hold her. I liked the way her body felt underwater.

She just wanted to race and would dart above and below me like a beam of light while I flabbily gasped and flabbily thrashed. Once, I placed my foot squarely on her chest and pushed. But I went nowhere. She wooshed back in the water's slowness.

She jumped out of the pool and went to the women's locker room without looking back. I found her later in the bleachers watching toddlers play softball on a truncated diamond.

So I have kicked a woman. But I was thinking long-term.

Sorry you're feeling at a dead end. I hope it passes soon. It's not true you are no good. I would bet my life on it. You're one of the best I know at many things. If only you could get my television up and running again after last night's storm, then you'd be perfect.

I got quite drunk and talked too much at a big dinner with seven friends from out of town. Since the breakup with Robin there was a brief encounter with a girl who yelled at me for calling her puss a riddle. I was on my knees when I said it. I was still on my knees at the side of her bed when she stomped off, shaking the wood floor, causing a battery-operated penis to roll out and nudge my knee like a pup. Does this sound like I'm explaining death to a three year old.

The heat holds on here in its last days. I spend much of each day worrying that the unseasonable weather is leading my instruments astray. I ponder this while taptapping the scabs on my arm.

I feel rabbit-hearted. No booze in the bungalow. I don't know if there are hookers at the Vortex conventions. It's getting harder and harder to tell who is charging for sex these days. I don't know if the women are changing or if it's me. Women get that total lack of respect for a man if the current is seen to sweep him and his hand grasps in an unsure way. That's it, the man is finished to them. A pallid vole patting the ground for his lost spectacles. It's like cats and water. They'll sit in the sink appearing to wait for you to turn on the faucet, but when you do, they want no part of it.

I feel a little guilty sometimes just sending you thoughtless scraps. But I know you don't mind and I know you welcome any little thing I do. Because we are both of us alone. It has been striking me again and again lately. You have to get hit or at least swung at constantly if you want to get close to the Core. And when in close cling, take little, crippling shots.

I woke early and thought I should do something noble. Get my driver's license for this state. A groaning, howling subway car dropped me in an unknown part of town. I went to where the office was supposed to be, but there was a sign saying it had moved. It gave the new address, a street I'd never heard of, and I set off for it. After a couple blocks I couldn't remember the name of the street, not that I was about to ask anyone. I kept walking, half-thinking that I would walk all the way home (an overly long and unfootful way) or randomly be seen by a friend with a car. I had a 1:00 P.M. appointment with a plumber at my house (it was 12:30 P.M.).

I walked aimlessly and it began to rain. Why do I do such things.

I hope the answer is that I embrace life with abandon. But I fear the truth is that I'm irresponsible. The same reason I had to have a stranger clean my mouth. I hailed a cab as a life-changing event and when I got home, the plumber had cancelled.

I've been painting what I consider to be landscapes viewed from the side window of a car. What you picture when I say that is probably better than what it actually is. I get full of steam. Paint is expensive. I justify it like a drug binge. I can do thirty bucks worth of Cadmium Red today. It's not like I'm going to do it every day.

I can't believe that rabbit-crusher said what she said about your body. Believe me, there has been nothing but steins thwacked on tables of approval from all the men I know that know you.

I called her rabbit-crusher because she's the type of woman who could walk into a room and stand on a rabbit without noticing.

A kid came around offering to clean the windows for free, a promotional thing. I kept saying no and he kept saying, *If I was going to give you 100 dollars, would you take it.* He ruffled around in his pockets each time as if searching for the C-note. Poor kid.

There's also a cat that looks through my glass door at night until it has compiled enough stats. And a squirrel that checks on me in the mornings, perched on the fence outside the window. He's got orange humanesque hands like a G.I. Joe doll. I wouldn't say he is fat but more so than most squirrels. He travels with a cooler. You'd like him.

I asked my neighbor, *Do you know what those birds are that are everywhere, are they eagles.* She said, *No, those are grackles. They're like crows. They're pests.* I said, *I'm talking about the birds with the four foot wingspan.* She said, *No, I don't know what you're talking about.*

They are circling everywhere and she's never seen them. She doesn't use her neck. She only acknowledges things that come at her head on. And she's one of those people that answer your question before you even get through it. And the answer always begins with No, even if it's Yes. Or worse, No no no.

The night is so separate from the day. Two platforms with no bridge between. You've got to leap, grasp and scramble from one onto the other. It can still surprise. When I visit other cities I sometimes think, Hey—they have days here, too.

We are building a bridge, though, aren't we.

I hope you are feeling as rich as a yolk in an egg white.

You are my camping cup, my strong back, my properly folded flag.

If you feel you are out of your league in attempting to describe something then it probably doesn't exist. There is no good vs. evil. I can see this most clearly at a boxing match. The crowd may attach good and evil to the opponents in a vain attempt at justifying their emotions. If they take pleasure in seeing a man fall, he must be a bad man.

I'm more inclined to having a favorite and an underdog. It gives me someone to root for in a fight I know nothing about. This is something that can be quantified, defined, and is mutable.

I've had a struggling few weeks. Drunk in the afternoon and jumping rope in the evening, maybe still drunk, as these are the easiest, spongiest workouts of all time. And after, when I am flayed out on the couch, is the only time I see the one star visible through the window so small and high.

Why did I build it so small and high.

I figure you might as well charge up the precipice feigning ignorance. It's not a crime if your case is strong. Keep the eyes averted and get it done. I am not one who believes that we all should be punished for the indiscretion of the individual. For the rest of our lives to labor under these laws that were made because some rich old dame's lapdog got run over by a Conestoga wagon. So we suffer speed bumps every ten feet (god knows I would be going a hundred miles per hour in every parking lot if I could), colonial liquor laws, and no sodomy in Snoqualmie.

Last night my eye swelled up and was all bloodshot and was the same this morning. Where's my cut man. Some kind of flu cold is trying to get into my body but I'm not going to let it.

There's a monkey in the works about my neighbor's sexuality. I was convinced she was gay based on bursts of inspirational hand clapping but yesterday she mentioned a boy she used to see. But the word boy from a woman of years gave it an archaic, mythical quality. So this boy—had he winged feet and a chariot of gold, mayhaps.

I went to the new shopping mall, they are like big empty aquariums where young girls learn to swim without water. Where the people fish. I was way too old to be in high school today.

How come naps are so much sweeter than regular sleep. Because it's the type of sleep that you can't resist, it just takes you. As opposed to the praying and the grassy teas.

People next door are watching TV on their front porch. Strange, huh. I don't think I've ever watched TV outdoors. I have chosen them as my surrogate family to spy on and drop myself into.

I really ought to call my grandmother.

I hope you got a roll with dinner that wasn't on the menu.

And that you are answering your walkie-talkie with a smile.

That's a lot of activity you described. I can hear pie pans clattering and dog toenails ticking. You had all that fun and now you've got the place to yourself. Sounds like you got it pretty good. For how long.

Robin is also one of those people. I hate to say it, but everyone I meet since has slept with her. I was at this party a while back...the whole room it seemed. Well, it was just one person. But he was pretty tall.

She used to undress in the closet. When I talked to her while she was in there, I felt like I was on a shrink's couch. But I didn't fill the silences often. I didn't want to make it feel like any kind of tradition.

Her parents' dog looked at me like I had beaten it years ago. Come to think of it, her whole family looked at me like I'd beaten them once. I wanted to take a ventriloquist dummy to those family dinners and not say a word. Just have the thing propped on my knee with both of us looking around wild-eyed.

She had misconceptions of me—thought I was neat and organized. She held on to this despite my protestations, then got angry if I left a cup out.

I would like to go back and tell her family that you love me. They gave me a fiddle for Christmas. She had told them I could play. Maybe I had told her I could play at some point. I can't. But I know how to hold it so I held it and said, *This is how you hold it*.

You're right, I can "prattle on" in my letters. A more supportive friend would have described me as "on fire." In my defense...I have no defense. I love you.

I would get you a personal assistant if I could. Like in the Russian novels where everyone, no matter how poor, had a maid and a butler. A maid to serve you a stale crust of bread and a butler to announce that it was ready.

I also tend to flip on the TV first thing to get the news since I don't get a paper delivered by a freckle-faced kid. On a bicycle. Little Billy. I used to be that kid. Tossing the paper in an arc into the void of now.

I could explain to you all the machinations of what I have to do in the next few weeks but it's so interwoven I'd be sending you a Persian rug. There is a Vortex convention and a visit to HQ.

The people across the way have put up a big picture of Jesus in their window. He's staring into my apartment. Somedays it's a painting, somedays it's a photograph.

I hope someone drops a burlap sack of cash on your doorstep. And that you will undo a button on your poncho.

I have to go back to the dentist. He's going to give me his master plan and the extractions begin sometime thereafter. I'm not sure how I will eat the universe then. A dream. I haven't dreamt in a month. It only means it's being stored up for the big one. I didn't really understand your question about who did I think was the more direct of the two of us. I understand the question but couldn't find an opening we could both fit through. Beyond that I feel you are steering this boat. On your back in a sundress with your bare foot on the tiller, yes, but steering nonetheless.

I don't really have proof that the tall feller slept with Robin. I don't even think he actually did. I just meant that he would have if he could have. The vigorous handshake and all that.

You're right about hard work. Or your thoughts match mine, at least. But I feel overwhelmed with the everyday things that insist on my attention. And under-whelmed. When faced with everything sometimes the best course of action is nothing.

Too short for even you. I'll write more soon. I have to go to bed now in the dark with bourbon (the drink, not the stripper).

I have never cried in the shower. That's a woman thing I think.

What happened to your heartbeat. Tell me soon as it's not a good place to have a question mark.

When was the last time you dressed for Halloween and what were you. I have not done it in my adult life. I remember what my last costume was. I was 15 and insisted on dressing up as a baby. There was a contest. Bed sheet as diaper, lipstick on cheeks in two red circles, a bonnet made out of Christmas wrapping. Big teddy bear in tow. But I refused to shave the dark down on my upper lip which I had been cultivating for a year. Certain I would take first place. Baffled when I didn't even get an honorable mention. Didn't they see me.

I am bathing regular. I am making suppers with more care. I am driving to theaters I never go to alone. I am making evenings of things.

Work progresses in utter silence. That is, I don't hear the voices of doubt. I read an article about a town where people were falling down a lot.

A few nights ago a friend asked, *Where are the women.* We cruised by the place we thought they were. It was dead. We cruised by a couple other bars. By the way, cruising means slowing down and looking in the door or at the people on the sidewalk. I don't even know what we want to see. What would make us stop and go in.

I think my buddy would like to see a bar three-quarters full with a male/female ratio of twenty/eighty. Me, I'd like the bar to be near empty. With Emma Bowlcut sitting by herself, smoothing out an empty straw sleeve.

We could make an evening of things.

I really need you to be behind me and not calling me a wolf. Though I have been in a savage mood. I got sick and lying in bed alone for uncountable days gave me time to mull and muse and stew with a weakened mind.

Excuse my absence, the mailbox was out of reach. Even the radio—which sped through a couple centuries of sonatas, fugues, death waltzes—was too distant. When I finally got up I was not depressed, I was angry. You're a fucking idiot was the refrain. No matter how small the act, like burning my hand on a hot plate (not a hotplate —things haven't got that bad yet)!

I was holding myself responsible for things beyond my control. But I'm getting out of it by sleeping in the guest room on the little bed. And writing you from the guest room. And taking readings from here. And feeling better. But I haven't been talking to anyone and I think that's dangerous, like a country without a language. I haven't had a live conversation in over two weeks. I fantasize like a bastard.

Oh, there was the one guy. A talker. Talked at me. Maybe this is the cause of all this. Threw his words like melting darts and watched me like a fifty cent movie.

I read your letter while the eggs were spitting and the coffee dripping, then came back to it. Between you and me I can only be so forgiving of someone who would be moderately cruel and claim it was a stopgap for the geyser of cruelty within them. But I'm guilty of it, too.

Bye-bye bicuspids. You don't want a necklace out of those things. I'm not anxious about what must be done. Extractions. It's not in my nature to think about the future until after it has happened. I almost stop and buy cigs after seeing the dentist. The fancy tobacco store is right next door. Instead, I let myself have a cup of coffee after supper. Like an old man or a European.

I talked to my grandmother. She claimed I was her son.

I tried to explain that I was her son's son. We talked for a long time and I'm not sure she knew who I was for any of it. Which made me doubt she was who she was.

Work is a lead ball hammered deep into the ground. I ought to lighten up is what your letter said to me.

How's your urinary tract.

It was really good to get your last letter. I was happy. I should have known you'd have something sharp to say, more interesting than the things other people would say. It is sadly humorous to see foolish men think they are lapping you with their wit and cunning. The scanning of my face for muscle reaction as he brought the needle of the dart closer and closer was exactly what was missing from my account. Seems you were there more than I was.

I used to dread giving my order to a waitress as a kid. It went around the table in slow motion, everyone else ordering, and when is she going to get to me. And then everyone's looking at me. It's funny how intently people watch other people ordering, as if it's going to illustrate how to deal with desire.

I also wonder about the volume at which people speak. How does one choose their personal volume level. What I really want to know is why do some people talk so much louder than necessary.

The fights have not been landmarks. Two in a row only went one round. And some company now throws candy at the crowd. First they try to hand you some as you walk in and then they circle and pelt them at you in your seat. People go crazy for anything you throw at them. A 60-year-old man diving on the floor and ripping his pants for a five cent lollipop.

I think a lot of the people at matches get in free somehow. I look around and can't imagine these people even know where they are. Why does it feel like I'm the only one who should be there. Everywhere I go, it feels like this.

I don't invite friends along. They'd be into the candy and the blood you can see. I'm more interested in the blood you can't see.

A boxer who had already fought was standing at the edge of the crowd with his wife. She went to the bathroom, leaving him with her purse, just standing there with her purse, still in his fight clothes. He may as well have slipped on her stilettos. Those lucky enough to be seated behind him were able to exchange quick smirks, but the poor saps facing him had to hold it in.

I'm almost always for the challenger. The big gloating champ rarely appeals to me. Unless they are just completely, undeniably, seamlessly crushing. There is a pipe-wire feller who I've seen get knocked the hell out every time he fights. He usually explodes in anger when the ref ends the match. He was there last night. Got knocked the hell out. Got up before the count but the ref wouldn't let him continue. He exploded briefly but then starts smiling and hugging everyone. Music plays while the MC prepares to announce the winner. He's the loser and he is bopping frenetically in the center of the ring until they drag him out. He could be seen the rest of the night making the rounds with a big smile, yelling unintelligible praise, dancing and drinking beer.

In another fight, a boxer who kept getting warned and penalized for low blows was disqualified. His kid, maybe 12 years old, jumps in the ring and tries to get to his father so he can understand their relationship has not been defeated. He can't reach him because of the mass of people. The kid lunges at the ref and does a head fake in his direction. Then he runs out of the ring bawling with red face and purple tongue. Mother and others restraining him and holding him for fifteen minutes.

Later they all walked off together like a family of geese thinking of giving up flying.

Tonight there is more. There is one fighter I'm looking forward to. Big feller. Big. He doesn't feint. He plants his feet like the king and queen on a chess board. His opponents almost laugh because they can't believe the power.

Oh, I am going to be in town fairly soon for the Vortex convention. I can bring a friend. If you can't go, I will hire a chimp.

Can I borrow one of your dresses for him, though. I have

my pride. Late nights, I imagine I will be scratching on your door, at least.

I'm not requiring you to go looking for fun or to set up anything.

I will only be there a few days. But if it's alright with you can we take the breakfast dates one morning at a time. One testy, shoe-throwing morning at a time. If I don't get my eight hours—I will eat your children. I think you should come but only from my own vantage point, because I so desperately hate routine and love change. So I'm assuming that's good for you, too. Even though it may well not be. All I'm thinking is the so much that you want to do will be there when you get back.

I don't think there is a cure for ants. Nothing from this world can enter or alter their world. If you find something let me know. I've been meaning to read a book on ants. Knowing only that they dwell in the Vortex but need some crucial thing from us. To be crushed, scorched or drowned if they become too established or showy.

It's good you are out of the sour. I feel half in and half out of it myself. Heading out. There is the sense that the imps of existence are backfooting it just out of my scope. The buildings they hide behind were built without hope.

A great man once said to me, *All we can do is try to do the work as best we can. That's it.*

I think I'm pretty good at keeping a secret, because I hate people. But I'm not too good at supplying them. So give it to me.

My voice has a strange accent lately. Wistful Korean grocer, chiding a pyramid of pomegranates.

HQ wants me to come check in so I will be setting off soon. No convention for me. I was on the phone with them and they kept asking me if I was alright. I kept saying, *Yes, I'm fine.* They said, *Why don't you come on up.* Figure it'll be a three-day drive. I will probably only be there for a day or two.

I got a postcard from my dental hygienist. She said it was time for my six-month cleaning and that she missed my beautiful smile. It was handwritten. I was in such a mood for a second I thought she might mean it. It was the only mail I got. And they didn't mention the fact that I haven't scheduled my surgery.

I'm suddenly sick of trying to put anything into words. If words are currency then all I got is small change. There are boards to be paced. Trod. And ghostly spinning micrometers to be palmed and re-palmed, palmed and re-palmed.

There are a couple of very slow drip sounds developing. Behind the walls in a little corner I can't get to. The fights last night were good. At the end of one, the trainer came out and yelled at his fighter after he won. Before he even cut his gloves off. He said, *If that's how you're going to box, you might as well give it up. I'm serious.*

And people ask me why I love boxing.

I saw a show about the animals of Judea. They showed how the young ibex—a goat/deer combo with someone else's headgear— jump in the air and pair up to ram their flat hornless heads. They jump like that in preparation for scaling mountain faces.

You're under stress. You are not the owner of a bad brain. It's all in the great plan: if she is having rough days, fuck her sleep with nightmares.

I still feel that you have it, the touch.

The Touch.

You see this is only your little ibex pal you're pairing up against to butt heads with until we both hop up the mountain. That's all this is.

I have to go to HQ. I don't have a choice. It's essential. I'll only be there for a day or two and then we can see each other.

It smoothed me out to read your letter. Despite your strife you are so tender to me. I was certain it was going to be a Vicodin night as I needed some pinning down. But I lost that feeling when I read what you wrote.

I don't know where we stand. And that is an eternal life for us. A feeling like emptying your lungs to sink to the bottom of a lake and squishing the mud underfoot then coming back to shore with clean feet.

So I guess I'm saying that we stand at the bottom of a lake, holding hands and working our toes. And we will someday swim to the shore with clean feet.

Everything I've done today could have been done by a bear. The long seasoned sleep. The lumbering out of bed. Tearing at a hard roll dipped in honey. And then sprawling lazily in the grass where the sun hit. I was going to take a bath but decided that would have been too much bear activity, so I showered. Or will in a bit. If I took a bath I think I would hunker down, expecting Emma Salmon to swim by so I could scoop her up.

Saw a lone deer at yesterday's sunset. It looked down the road with an expression as if waiting for something in particular. Antlers. That deer had a nice face. Like it would help you out in a jam if it could.

We are both going away. I had thought it was only me. I will now be paying more attention to what you will pack than to what I will.

Last night the wind was blowing fierce and temperatures were dropping fast. The blind knocked a glass item off the sill. I knew it would happen but left the glass item there anyway. The bedroom door was slamming open and shut. Fell asleep and woke with a scream while staring at a dark spot on the wall. When lightning flashed I saw the horizon on all four walls. Your silhouette on each. I knew then that I know exactly what it would feel like to stand before you again. With your nose moving as it does.

When I got up I noticed several complete outfits of clothes in piles on my floor. As if a group of men had dropped them and gone out into the storm naked.

If you think of something, do you stop to write it down.

PART TWO

I'm up at HQ now. I woke up excited by the rain-slicked roads. I wanted to hear the hiss of tires. But I only drove to the airport, stopping to buy fresh duds and a duffle bag. HQ said I oughtn't drive all the way here. They're trying to reverse the Vortex temporarily, as an exercise, to see if they can. They're talking like it's imminent. Feels like a publicity stunt. I don't know what it's all about. I would hate to think I had anything to do with this. I would hate to think that a large reason for living would end.

But I could find a reason to live in any situation. Siamese fighting fish can live in a water buffalo's hoof print filled with rainwater. We live in a hoof print, dreaming of where the next foot fell.

Don't use the address on the envelope, I'll only be here a few days. There was some feller waiting for me outside my cabin this morning. You know the type —pretends not to know you, but he's the one coming up and doing the talking. And his face shows that everything he's saying isn't what he truly wants to say. You can see it just there in the cheek. I wanted to deck him.

I could become a boxer. Easy.

You might as well start sending your letters here. I will be stuck here for longer than I thought. I slipped, cracked my head on the shower wall. Was hoping for a lump but not a scratch on this infernal orb. The elfin doc insisted I stick around for tests.

I have been mostly dull lately. Like a butter knife. And hoping to find, when called upon, something more in my arsenal than a butter knife. Unless my opponent is actually butter. Then I would be fine. Room temperature butter.

I sometimes see a shortcoming in myself, how little patience or understanding I have for many people with the way they act. I am able to see the fragility in some, but I only have so much time to wade through their manipulations and traps and draining behavior. Some people think I'm heartless in leaving others to suffer their own selves. The whole trip has been depressing for reasons I would probably never tell anyone. Ego tings. You know I try to be strong for you. Still, it's exhilarating and exhausting to meet so many people and have to be on. And at the end of the day there is a canteen meal. One long table. One night I made a joke about changing my diaper between courses. It bombed. Not a ripple. There are levels to compatriotism.

I bought a suit. The first non-secondhand suit I've ever bought. First day I wore it was on the plane trip here. It's time to stop wearing other people's clothing. I also bought some boots. The shoe man in The Bootery said, *You have to have attitude to wear these!*

Wore them on the plane, too.

There was a girl, Emma junior, sitting across the aisle from me. She had long thin legs in jeans and virgin white sneakers. Her grandfather next to her and another girl of her age to his right. Probably her best friend. She and I were both admiring Jr.'s leg and shoe for the hope found there. The way the jean leg went to the perfect height above the shoe. It was satisfying to look at. Eventually her eyes wandered across the aisle to my boots. I was ready for her. She took them in. They are not of the fashion. They were unfamiliar to her. No one in her school wore them. Did they mean something or nothing. We both looked at my right foot but before too long our eyes went back to the white shoe and thin leg and stayed there.

I found myself rosy reading your portrayal of love. It is sure-footed and goes against petty squabbling. I still want to know about the things you couldn't tell me but said you one day would.

It's 12:34 A.M. The time on the clock feels significant, as it often does here. As if the numbers are looking for the right combination to unlock me. Look, look, how much more obvious can it be.

I'm lying down. I might as well go to sleep.

Yesterday I remembered the time I was staying at an ex-girlfriend's house, while her husband was at work. Have I mentioned Becky Plaits. I was attempting to take a late morning nap after some days away from sleep. It was a small, open apartment and Becky was trying to keep her boy from talking. He knew how to talk but he hadn't learned to whisper. I lay there listening, not considering myself disturbed by his talking—being awake for whatever reason I had been awake for two days already.

She kept trying to explain how to whisper. She had about given up. After a long pause when the mother sat in frustration, he whispered the word sleep, and I slept.

There is a reason ice is slippery. Did anyone laugh at you. I have an inability to help anyone who has fallen. To witness injects me with a paralytic joy. If someone falls in front of me, you've never seen such a smile in your life. I'm tickled by the chance that they are learning something.

Those falls encapsulate half my studies. If we can remember how we feel when our footing was gone and the ground had not yet accepted us.... I took another spill yesterday. I froze mid-air, as if my life became a complete circle there and any additional movement would shatter it.

The elfin doc is concerned. Painted wooden steps leading out of the cabin. A smattering of beaded rain. I was wearing the impractical treadless booties that Robin used to say I looked hot in. And I was carrying four boxes of notes and readings and data reels. Slipped on the first step and rode all the way down on my coccyx. I watched it all in great detail and wished I could take a reading every time I bounced. I thought, I wonder if he's going to hit his head.... The boxes and all inside them went flying, reels rolling.

Reached bottom. Looked around. I saw elfin doc's glasses flashing behind a window. Got up. No injuries. No physical proof. I did a little shuffle like that boxer who always gets knocked out, then re-spooled the dewy reels.

I associate those types of falls with childhood. I was constantly flying off my bike for attempting the impossible. Jumping a ditch. Riding through a rocky creek. Knees skinned daily. Concrete like a cheese grater on skin. Pain was a fresher and more bracing sensation then. Lemon juice. These days it's more nuanced, like lime juice.

I will probably leave here soon. I could visit you, float in like a cloud, real nimbostratus like.

So you hold on to those old memories like dream ingots, too. I don't need to know the specifics. It's enough to know you are holding them. Although I may ask someday. Deathbed request. We are alike in ways that only a scalpel could prove. As you can maybe tell, I am not there with you.

I fell again even after donning the regulation Vortex boots. The elfin doc did a thorough check up. I'm as healthy as an ox, but they want me to stay here so they can observe me. I've been transferred to a different cabin, one with no furniture, so I sit on the floor. If I stand up and walk a straight line people gasp and applaud. I walked to the little commissary and it was as if I were their child going to his first day of school. Hankies to their mouths. I play it up for them with little dips and slips and dashes to the edge of the abyss.

When I was a child, my mother used to beg me to take a bath, but once I was in there she'd have to beg to get me out. I am looking for drinking partners once I get out of here. But I can't think of a way to meet up with your pal that wouldn't be awkward. I have a past vision of meeting his wife, but it may be conjured from things you have said about her. I can see her. But I can't imagine in what capacity I would have met her.

I can see us briefly shaking hands and parting. But right after that I see myself in rags running through a sewer with rats, so I'm not sure how trustworthy the memory is.

They've been through my notes and nodded. They suck the air from my room when they step into it. As soon as they leave, I snap back.

I've been crawling.

I could probably walk, but I've been crawling.

You see the undersides of things. The undersides of things haven't changed much since I was small. A table with thick black bolts. A dresser with a patch of yellowed paper that looks like it should have fallen off twenty years ago. A lengthy equation written on it in intricate, illegible penmanship.

I understand you are frustrated with me. My inability to visit you. I tend to look too long at the intricate, illegible messages pasted around me. I am doing my best to get out of here. I thought you'd be the first to say I had superpowers. I'm glad you didn't. My powers are a frenzied patience, lackadaisical perseverance, and despairing optimism.

Do women get hairier with age. I know some old women have the face fuzz, but how common is that. I tell you, I'm growing hairier by the minute. Still nothing on my back yet, but I don't check that often.

We need something we can send into nothing. I mean we have it, I'm just saying we need it. Acknowledgement is half the battle. The other half is old plain combat.

The elfin doc asked what I wanted out of life. I said, *One of those big desk blotter calendar things.* Because I've wanted one for about twenty years and never gotten around to buying one. And lately it has felt that there is too much coming up to store in my feathery head. The doc brought me one minutes later. I started to enter information I'd been carrying on various scraps of paper. Half the dates had passed. But I was so excited about having the calendar that I entered the expired events, too.

I'm glad you're getting some good done. I am molting. I'm not exaggerating when I say I mostly stare.

People look at animals and ask, incredulous, *What are they thinking all day as they eat their nuts and berries.*

Look within, my friend! The Vortex rages!

When I woke the doorknob was on the floor and a wet wind blew through. I found the screws and a screwdriver and set about to fixing it. It should have taken ten minutes. It took me two hours! The screws would not go in. It had me cursing the day monkeys invented tools. Or is that too contemporary a cultural reference for you.

I almost threw the screwdriver through the window several times. But now the knob is back on, slightly loose. I never for one second thought it would be a difficult task. If there is one thing I have it is a buoyant, unreasonable hope about things I haven't experienced.

My parents taught me to always lie about my profession. But up here I can't. It's all on the table.

I took a Vicodin yesternight and my breadline blood turned chalky white in its honor. I made a really good omelet, saluted my reflection in the window a couple dozen times and then slept like a teenager.

It's overcast and misty and a crow is jiving with the jay's nest.

I need some good affection and to squeeze a denim butt.

I climb up on the cabin roof sometimes to let the stars into my eyes. But once I am up there they seem farther away than when I am on the ground. There is a constellation that reminds me of your hipbone. I think I am trying to get closer to that bunch of light.

The other night I fell asleep with my head against the cool, mossy shingles. I could hear the scrabbling of mice or squirrels. I was certain it was old Orange Hands playing dice in the rain gutter.

I can feel the way your hips would fit into my hands perfectly, like a lifetime rifle or an overweight but well-groomed cat. Or a large-breed dog who rarely gets lifted but loves it sheepishly when it does. A foot finding a solid hold in a rock face where before there was none. And then for it to be covered in skin, what could be better. Child, take care of that hip.

When they say it's okay to leave here, I swear I'm coming straight to see you. I should have come to see you when it was easy.

I saw some sort of wildcat out my window. Too big and stripey to be a domestic stray. They're getting off the mountain since the Vortex tourist development began.

I hope that you are in the depths of something good. That that is why I have no mail from you.

I'm tired of hearing about my gray. One of the docs puckered his face up and said, *What have you done to your hair.* As if it were Bozo orange. As if it was something I'd done.

He was displaying on his desk a red pepper from his garden. I nabbed it on my way out of his office.

I think fish became humans because they didn't have any way to pistol whip each other.

This is the Unbowed. Post-op. I've got two dentist Vicodin in me. One penicillin, too. Who's going to go and get me yogurt cups and soup cans. This is opiate-fueled prose. Prose he says!

Doctor Caesar, the HQ dentist, wears one stud earring and square-toed shoes. The procedure was not too bad. I wouldn't dread doing it again. Him holding my jaw, the nurse holding my head up. I was comforted by the fact they deemed it a two-person job. Drills, needles, pliers. I wasn't under anesthetic but they were talking so quiet and conspiratorially it made me feel as if I was.

The one tooth was putting some awful gunk in my mouth. I am glad it is gone. It was causing me to nicker and sometimes bray. I think it was also putting something into my bloodstream as my skin smelled of sweet rot.

Battle Bean, I feel shot. My face has swollen up a little. Not the half a grapefruit you are probably banking on. I have lowered a flag or two, still I don't hear from you. I am unable to express the past couple days. Of where I have gone and what I have seen there. If the Vortex is unchanging, why take readings of it. Why not just let it be. But I guess it doesn't really let me be. If I let it, would it let me be.

I miss your moral reliability. I will write again soon.

My haircut routine is to be topless over the bathroom sink while I guide as much shorn hair as possible into a brown paper bag. It's a lot of work to keep it so short. It feels like duty. When does duty become not duty become not diligence or discipline become the wasted act.

It feels like the wasted act.

I'm going to let it grow.

I called the operator when I was small. My first unaided call. After a long silence I told her, *There's a robin in the back yard on a tree.* The words, *Is that right, Sugar* melted from her as if I was her favorite son.

I wonder if she ever thinks of me. I wonder what happened to that robin. No I don't. It's dead and festered away to nothing. But what happened to that phone, and that desire.

I am still on the floor for the most part. Last night clung to the beard for dear life. If I let go, would I whip crack to the ceiling and back. Woke bleary-headed and bleary-eyed and took some micro readings. Strictly off the record. The day moves as if shackled.

The wind is howling in the heater vent but the trees are petrified still. Here it must.

My dental hygienist sent me a vacation photograph of her family. They are all holding her horizontally. The husband in the ass region. I looked at it for way too long. Those cuffed shorts. It's been a long time between drinks.

I watched the news and thought that a language without a country is a perilous thing. I did a little coatimundi-style investigation around the crater's edge. Toed some pebbles in. They are still falling. I promise I will let you know when they touch ground.

I could become a short story writer. Easy.

You are still reading so high on the meter that some would doubt the meter was functioning properly. Not me.

Oh, I've taken in a pet. A three-legged dog. I think he might've lost a leg to one of the evacuating wildcats. Life will be alright, I think, with a three-legged dog.

I woke up naturally at 7:00 A.M. But then I got suspicious. So I thought backwards and remembered I'd heard a sound and that was why I was up. It was your letter, which had fallen through the slot. The dog looked at me and then hoppled to it and brought it over. We were happy to get word from you. Until we read it.

Yes, I remember Charlie. You have written of him in the past. You write like I don't know his routines and impressions. I'm sure he gets a very deep laugh out of you.

This letter meant to prove my understanding and patience, will only prove the opposite. I kind of thought that with what happened between you two that would be it for him in your life. This letter will thrash like an empty dishwasher running while the rabble in the next cabin over eat off my dishes. Jealousy writes its own letters.

Why do some people get away with so much shit, do whatever they want, and people keep letting them back in. He talks a good line. That's what saves these people. And they probably have a more efficient heart than I do. That's what really saves these people.

I know you're going to see him again and what we all (you both) went through will be used to his benefit. It will be an in for him where it should be an out. I'm doing the one thing I asked myself not to do, which is to write without picturing your face.

This is what it took. I was wondering what it would take to get me training in earnest to box. I have the impetus now. If I see Charlie, I want to be able to knock him out. He will probably raise his head and ring like a bell.

Don't make me go into that dark shack alone.

I just got word that they want to patent and mass produce my spine. That would bring some money in. But they're saying the process would destroy my spine and I'd have to have a replica inserted. Their argument is that I'd be happier with the new spine anyway. The fools.

They showed me a clipping from a newspaper saying I'm the roughest toughest son of a bitch since Icarus. That no one has gotten to such heights or depths and been able to hold the hand steady to document it. But it was an English newspaper so it doesn't really count. I showed them my method of getting around when I'm floor-bound —somersaults! Struck dumb by the obviousness. Them.

I am leaving this place tonight when it gets quiet. I am not sure where I am going to go. I think it's good, despite what they say, to hold the pain in sometimes. As if there is nothing to learn from letting the broken-winged bird flap in the ashes of your fireplace a couple of wing beats past your rescue reflex.

PART THREE

I have been driving around. No resting place. I've got a medicine ball in the passenger seat, all sorts of fitness gadgets scattered in the back. Pushing against resistance. That's what it's all about. It started with push-ups to get myself upright. Now that I have learned what I can about dropping to the ground, I want to teach my method to others by knocking them down. That force that was pinning me, I want for myself. I'm going back to that boxing gym.

The micrometers got smashed with the first few blows I threw into the gut of the heavy bag. I had taped them to my hands before putting the gloves on and punched until my fingers were bloody, torn and raw.

My trainer is very, very impressed. I mean unimpressed. I walked in there thinking he would see something in me. The seed. Of greatness. No dice.

He teamed me up with a noiseless, sweet, Latina manatee. Luisa Cabello. Not to spar, just to help each other out. She wraps my hands. It might be love.

Trainer wouldn't tell me when I could get in the ring. But I have heard talk around the gym of some after hours mango jango. Fights off the book. That's what I'm spoiling for.

Eight of us stayed behind after the gym had shut for the night. Four of us would fight, two would be corner men, one would referee, and one would be the cut man. I thought there should have been two cut men but there wasn't.

I wanted to go first, but they assigned me to the second bout. I watched the two men go at it. I was impatient. It was like looking at the solution to a long math problem. Or like walking in on the last two minutes of an epic movie.

I was paired up against that murderous lawyer with the black in his back and the hastily drawn face. I had seen him go against the heavy bag as if the last breath of air was in there and he needed it. When the first round started, I expected the lawyer, whose name was Garg, or something that sounded like Garg, to rush out on top of me and that would have been the end probably. But he didn't. He moved to the center of the ring and stood there, covered up, not throwing anything. I threw my first punches and he remained covered. So I continued, wailing on him for the entire round. His skin was chrome, a body ungiving. It was his first fight, too.

For the second round I figured he would open up and take some swings at me after getting a feel for what I could do but he didn't. The same as the first, he stood in defensive posture. Taking pictures they call it. I hit his arms, I hit his gloves, I hit the side of his head and all the parts of his torso that I could. The bell rang to signal the end of round two and he went back to his corner. I watched his shadow-back retreating.

The only times I got to see his face was at the beginning of a round before he put his gloves up and at the end when he took them down. It was as if he was holding up a mask. I wanted to see that face, to find some guidance in it. I was disgusted with him. It could be a strategy. At first I thought he was stupid. Then I thought he was crazy. Halfway through

73

the third round I started to think that maybe it was me that was crazy. Expending myself, returning to my corner a panting noodle while Garg sat calmly. He was fighting by not fighting and I was the loser against this bulky void. I knew he'd been taught to fight. Had spent hours and hours throwing hands at cushioned heads and speed bags and heavy bags. And now his moment has come and he hangs there like the heavy bag himself.

Then I drew blood. Lots of it. I don't know how. Maybe the laces of his gloves had lacerated his face. The blood was getting on my gloves and I was wiping it on the referee's shirt so that he wouldn't see it and stop the fight. At the end of the round the ref looked like a butcher in a sky blue shirt. The fourth was to be the final round.

My energy was low, but I thought of the countless others who had soldiered on in similar state. Garg stood in center ring covered up and I worked his body. Towards the end of the round he opened up. Like a great bird awakening and testing its wings with its feet still on the ground. The blows dazed me. I was surprised at how intimate it felt. Almost affectionate, if affection was something unpleasant. Within a few seconds I was on my back seeing stars.

When I came to everyone had left except the cut man. He was fiddling with something in the corner. When he saw me move he said, *Come on, we have to get out of here.*

I finally went to visit my grandmother in the nursing home. It was as if I couldn't go until I had a black eye. Until I had something to show her. We've never been too close. I feel she sees me as a misfit because I don't have a regular job and I'm not interested in anything like that. At reception I told them who I was and who I wanted to see. My grandmother, with a radiant smile, walked through one of the three doors that led off of the circular lobby. She had lost all the excess weight that she had carried throughout most of her life. It brought out the sparkle in her eyes. I handed her a bunch of flowers that I had bought from a man who was selling them out of a station wagon in front of the home.

We went to see her room. The bed looked like something that folds cars in a junkyard. There was a nightstand, two chairs, a TV mounted to the ceiling, and a bulletin board with photos tacked to it. We sat and talked for awhile about my drive, how long it took and how the traffic was.

She said there was a wine and cheese party in the rec room at 3:30 P.M. and we should go to that soon. She checked her watch and I checked mine.

I got up and stood before the wall of photos. When I saw someone I couldn't identify, I pointed to it and asked who it was. She looked at me and said a name I had always heard in the family. Then she pointed to a picture of a young man. She said, *You were never happy except when you were in that boat.* I, feigning scrutiny, looked at the old photo and said, *Oh no, that's Sam, isn't it.* Her husband. Dead.

Yes, that's you, Sam. She took my hand.

We continued looking at the photos. *And here you are again*, she said. Another picture of my grandfather. I saw no reason to correct her. We both checked our watches again and she said it was time to make our way to the party. A portly, disheveled minister with thinning gray hair askew, wearing a bright purple minister shirt, was cutting up a block of American cheese into small cubes and sticking toothpicks in them. It was only 3:15 P.M. but many residents were already there.

My grandmother introduced me around as her husband. Some of them smiled and said hello. Others looked at me like I'd done something wrong by waiting so long to show up. The minister asked me if I wanted red or white. He poured me half a glass of red. Less than half. Then, seeing that everyone who wanted a drink had one and that there were plenty of cheese cubes lined up, he left the room. A few residents immediately topped up their cups. My grandmother was talking to someone. I filled my cup.

From time to time I would hear the word husband and I'd scan around the room until I found someone looking at me with their glass raised. A toast. Some of the people served themselves again. Their voices were getting louder. I hadn't eaten much and the goofy juice was going straight to the dome. There was a low, medical hum. My grandmother disappeared from the room without me seeing her leave.

One of the men at the drinking table challenged another to an arm wrestling match. He kept saying, *C'mon* and clapping his hands with a sound that needled my ears. He kept doing it.

C'mon.

Clap!

C'mon.

Clap! Clap! Clap!

I stood up and moved towards the table, not sure what I was doing. The feller next to him relented and agreed to go against him. It was a relief. He couldn't clap while his hand was clasped in someone else's.

The match didn't last long. The clapper won. This increased his enthusiasm and the urgency with which he said, *C'mon* and clapped.

Another feller agreed to wrestle. Eyes were checking the door to see if the minister was coming back. Some of the residents appeared to be betting with cheese cubes.

This match took a little longer. Maybe the instigator was getting tired. But his winning streak and the crowd forming a circle around him pumped him up even more, made him more piercing. I could feel my face distorting. Then he locked eyes with me and said, *How about you, Son. You up for being beat by an old man.* I smiled and said, *Aww, well, no.*

He made a face like there wasn't enough time in this life for my kind and lifted his hands to rap them together. I grabbed a hand to stop him. It became a cock-eyed handshake as I said, *You're on.* The crowd applauded and made airy noises of lung.

Someone croaked, *On your marks!*, and we surged. I hadn't considered my chances of winning. I only knew I had to stop that clapping.

He gave a little bit, then regained. I gave a little bit, then regained. The match had already lasted longer than the others. The crowd was pressing in. My opponent grinned seriously. Brow scrunched and wine tongue popping out when he was falling behind. I had him within an inch of the table. His arm was trembling. I thought back on the boxing match I had been in. It would be really bad if I lost this, I thought. That would be no detail for an Emma letter. But it wasn't necessarily the winning of the match that would make you mine. It was something that I needed to find. A detail that only I could see and only you would understand. A detail that would lacerate your heart and send blood shuddering onto my face. I held him off but couldn't make the last inch. The crowd crackled like sparks off a wet wire. I looked around the room at the faces, to see if that's where the detail lay. A winged ant landed on the ridge of my opponent's greased black pompadour. A lady had her jacket on inside out. A brawny old man was wearing three watches and holding hands with a woman that had a clock tattooed on her arm.

Then I saw my grandmother had returned. Transfixed by the action and her mouth was moving slow, deliberate when she boomed, *That's my grandson!*

I pressed the hand to the table and with my eyes closed waited for the blood to rain down. Thunder cracked the clear day. No, someone had pushed the table over or it had collapsed. And the wine flew into a bright red arc above me.

Driving out through the desert for days. I found you in white petticoats. Several white petticoats under a peach colored dress. Your skin browned to the edge of redness. You were lying there on the hard cracked earth. An ocean once, no more.

But the water would return.

I lifted you up. You needed shelter. A metal roof. Anything to shield you from the sun. Your body as hot as a coal radiating, dispersing, glowing a heat like a long word. A word that never ends.

I carried you into a doorless and dim shack.